SESAME STREET

D0517778

Watch Out for Banana Peels

and Other Important Sesame Street Safety Tips

By Sarah Albee
Illustrated by Tom Brannon

A Random House PICTUREBACK® Book • CTW Books

Copyright © 2000 Children's Television Workshop (CTW). Sesame Street Muppets © 2000 The Jim Henson Company.
All rights reserved under International and Pan-American Copyright Conventions. Published in the United States by Random House, Inc.,
New York, and simultaneously in Canada by Random House of Canada Limited, Toronto, in conjunction with Children's Television Workshop.
Sesame Street, the Sesame Street sign, and CTW Books are trademarks and service marks of Children's Television Workshop.
Library of Congress Cataloging-in-Publication Data
Albee, Sarah.   Watch out for banana peels and other Sesame Street safety tips / by Sarah Albee ; illustrated by Tom Brannon.
"Featuring Jim Henson's Sesame Street Muppets." p. cm. — (A Random House pictureback book) SUMMARY: Officer Grover and Safety Deputy Elmo share
helpful safety tips about avoiding injuries, crossing the street, cleaning up spills, being careful in the kitchen and outdoors, and more.   ISBN 0-375-80482-X
1. Safety education—Juvenile literature. 2. Children's accidents—Prevention—Juvenile literature. [1. Safety.] I. Brannon, Tom, ill. II. Title.
III. Series: Random House pictureback. HQ770.7.A43 2000 363.1'07—dc21 99-15920   www.randomhouse.com/ctwbooks   www.sesamestreet.com
Printed in the United States of America January 2000 10 9 8 7 6 5 4 3 2 1
PICTUREBACK, RANDOM HOUSE and colophon, and PLEASE READ TO ME and colophon are registered trademarks of Random House, Inc.

SAFETY TIP #2: Always wear a helmet and safety gear when riding a bike or skating.

SAFETY TIP #3: Never pet a strange dog.

SAFETY TIP #8: Be sure to buckle up!